This book
belongs to

....

....

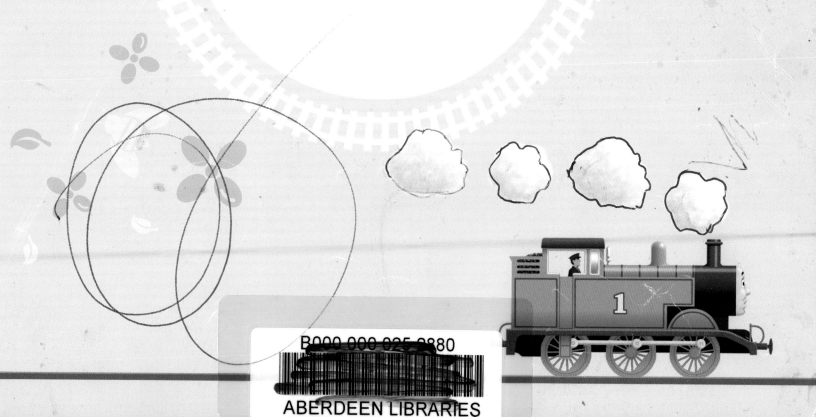

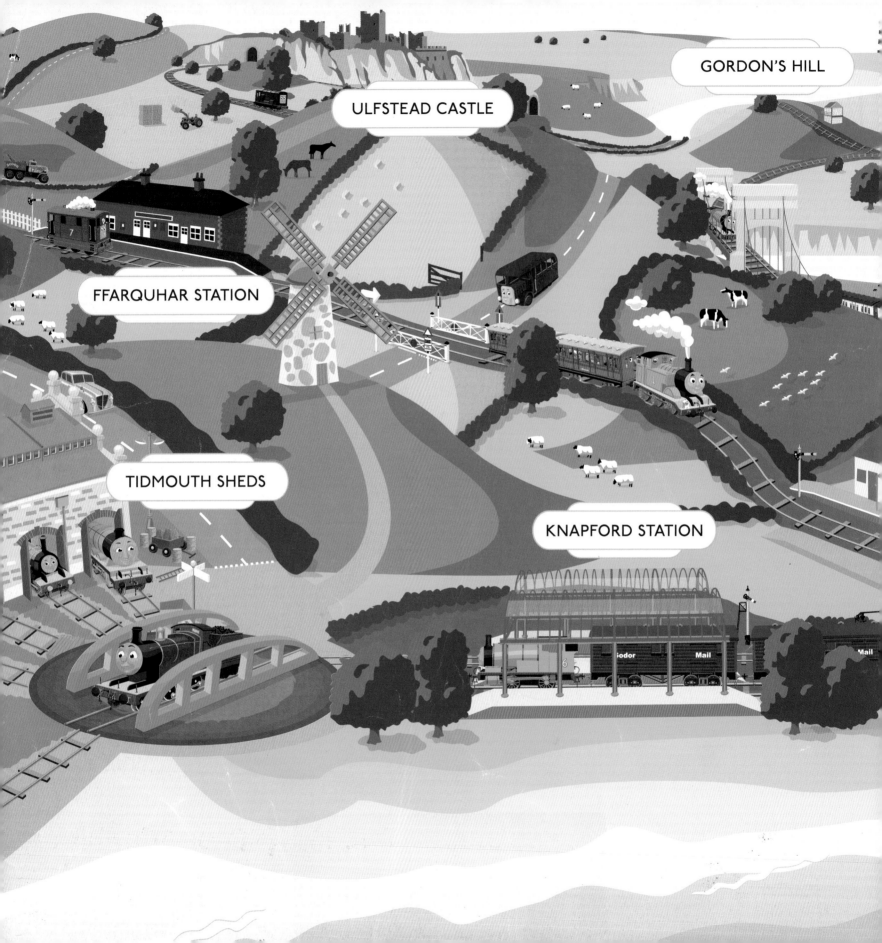

GORDON'S HILL

ULFSTEAD CASTLE

FFARQUHAR STATION

TIDMOUTH SHEDS

KNAPFORD STATION

BRENDAM DOCKS

CHINA CLAY PITS

DRYAW STATION

THE ISLAND OF SODOR

EGMONT

We bring stories to life

First published as Thomas & Friends The Spring Surprise in 2011
This edition published in 2019 in Great Britain by Egmont
The Yellow Building, 1 Nicholas Road, London W11 4AN

Written by Emily Stead and Helen Archer. Designed by Martin Aggett.
Illustrations by Robin Davies

 Thomas the Tank Engine & Friends ™

HiT entertainment   CREATED BY BRITT ALLCROFT

ISBN 978 1 4052 9291 7

70190/001

Printed in Poland

Egmont takes its responsibility to the planet and its inhabitants
very seriously. We aim to use papers from well-managed forests
run by responsible suppliers.

Stay safe online.
Egmont is not responsible for content hosted by third parties.

Thomas and the Spring Surprise

This is a story about a spring day when lambs were born on the farm and Thomas was given the chance to show what a Really Useful Engine he was …

One of Thomas' favourite things to do is to visit the farm. He loves to see Farmer McColl's sheep grazing in their field.

"Baa! Baa!"
the sheep would call.

"Peep! Peep!"
Thomas would whistle back.

One day, when Thomas was passing the field, Farmer McColl waved him over.

"Hello, Thomas!" said Farmer McColl. "I'm glad you're here. I have very special news. Some lambs are going to be born today."

Thomas was very excited.

"I can't wait to meet them!"

he peeped.

"Newborn lambs need
to have fresh straw,"
Farmer McColl explained.
"Can you go to the old
barn at Maron to
collect some?"

"Right away!"
Thomas puffed, and off
he went to the old barn.

Thomas wondered if there
was anything else the
lambs would like.

On his way, Thomas passed the bakery. He saw Percy loading his truck with freshly-baked bread.

"Maybe the lambs would like some bread," he puffed. "Percy, may I have some?"

"Of course!" said Percy and his crew loaded trays of bread into Thomas' truck.

Thomas steamed on cheerily, until he came to the garden centre where he saw James picking up colourful spring flowers.

Thomas was sure the lambs would like the flowers.

"May I have some for the lambs?"

Thomas asked, and James agreed.

Thomas was nearly at the old barn when he saw Charlie waiting at a signal.

"Hello, Charlie!" puffed Thomas. "I'm going to meet some newborn lambs today!"

"What fun!" chuffed Charlie. "I'm going to the dairy to collect cheese."

Thomas thought that the lambs might like cheese too, so he went with Charlie to have some cheese loaded into his truck.

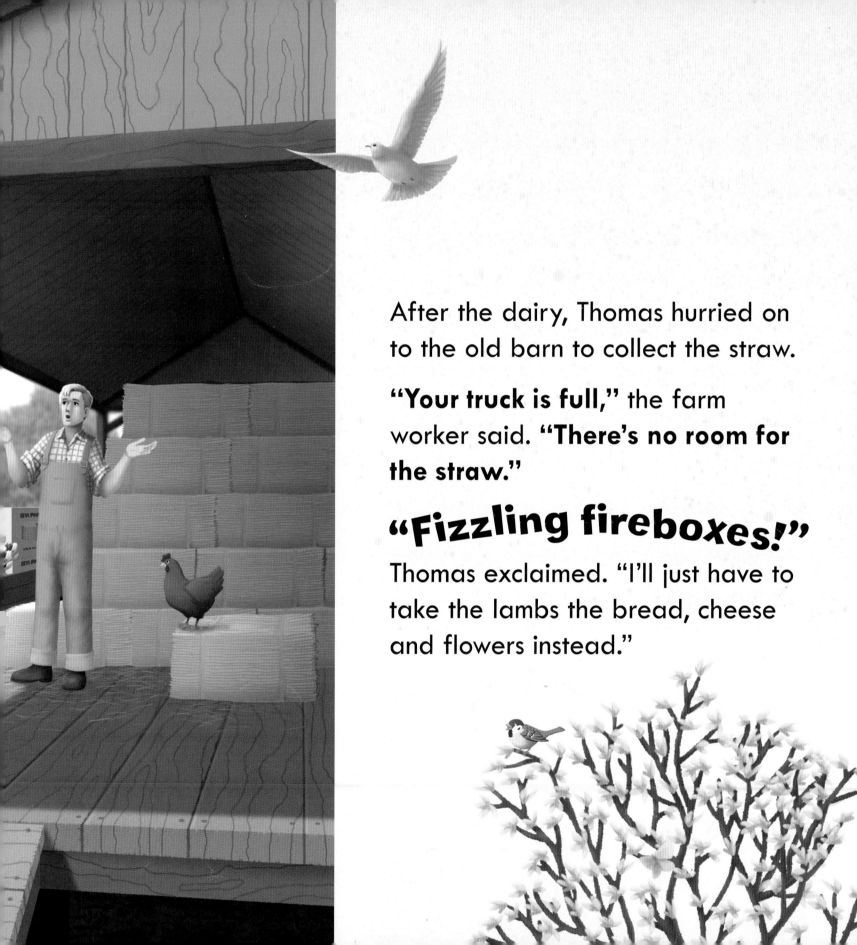

After the dairy, Thomas hurried on to the old barn to collect the straw.

"Your truck is full," the farm worker said. **"There's no room for the straw."**

"Fizzling fireboxes!" Thomas exclaimed. "I'll just have to take the lambs the bread, cheese and flowers instead."

When Thomas returned to the farm,
Farmer McColl was not happy to see
there was no straw in the truck.
"The lambs must have straw to keep
them warm," he said. **"And they'll be
born before the sun goes down!"**

Thomas felt very silly. "I'm sorry. I will
go and collect the straw straight
away!" he peeped.

Thomas raced back to the old barn, saying over and over to himself, "I must get the straw, there can be no delay. The lambs will be born by the end of the day!"

He **steamed** past Percy, refilling at the water tower, **whizzed** past James at a junction and Charlie at the station. There was no time to stop!

The sun was setting when Thomas arrived at the old barn.

"Hello again!" Thomas puffed to the Farm Worker. "Please can you load the straw into my truck? I must get it to the lambs before they get cold!"

The farm worker quickly loaded the straw bales and soon Thomas was on his way back to the farm.

Thomas steamed so quickly, his axles ached. "I must go fast, I mustn't delay. The lambs must have straw by the end of the day!" he sang.

When he reached the farm, he was so worried he would be too late.

"You're just in time," Farmer McColl smiled. **"The lambs have just been born!"**

Thomas was delighted he had arrived in time to meet the lambs.

The next day, Thomas took some school children to visit the new little lambs.

Farmer McColl laid out the bread, cheese and flowers and the children had a splendid spring picnic.

"I have a **surprise** for you, Thomas," smiled Farmer McColl. "I named this lamb **'Thomas'** ... after you!"

"Peep! Peep!"

Thomas whistled, happily.

"Baa! Baa!"

the lambs answered.

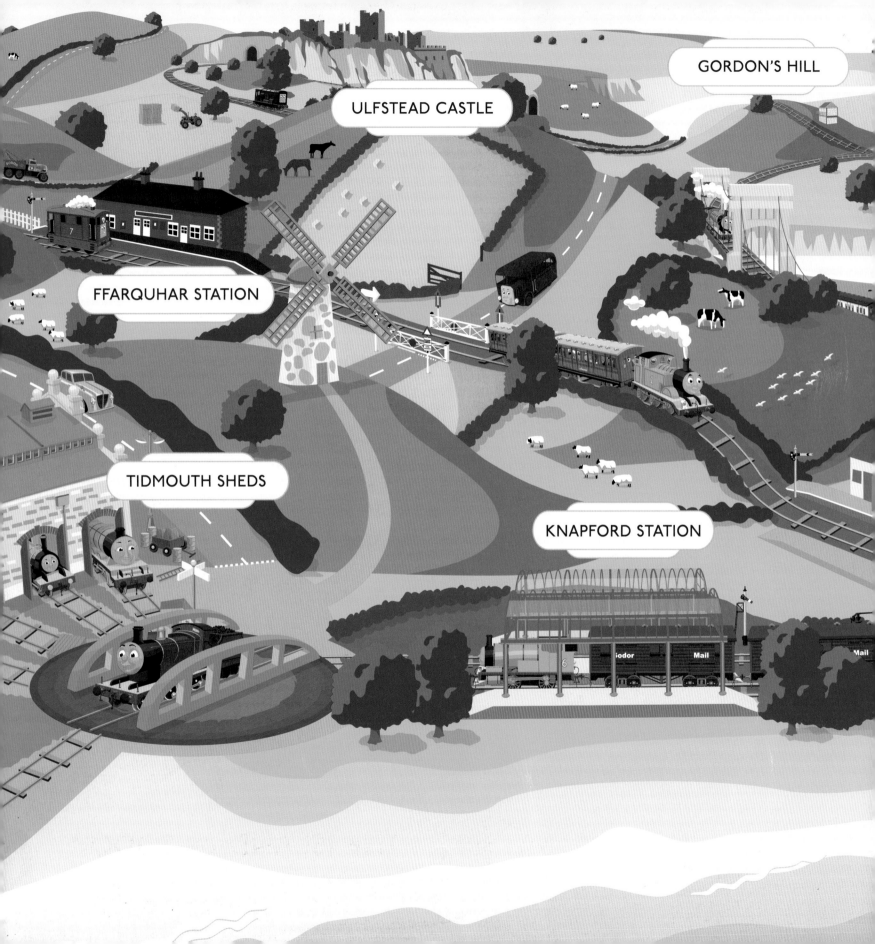

GORDON'S HILL

ULFSTEAD CASTLE

FFARQUHAR STATION

TIDMOUTH SHEDS

KNAPFORD STATION

BRENDAM DOCKS

CHINA CLAY PITS

DRYAW STATION

THE ISLAND OF SODOR

About the author

The Reverend W. Awdry was the creator of 26 little books about Thomas and his famous engine friends, the first being published in 1945. The stories came about when the Reverend's two-year-old son Christopher was ill in bed with the measles. Awdry invented stories to amuse him, which Christopher then asked to hear time and time again. And now for over 70 years, children all around the world have been asking to hear these stories about Thomas, Edward, Gordon, James and the many other Really Useful Engines.

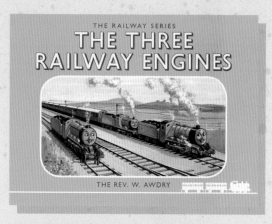

The Three Railway Engines, first published in 1945.

The Reverend Awdry with some of his readers at a model railway exhibition.